MONNIE HATES LYDIA

by SUSAN PEARSON · pictures by DIANE PATERSON

THE DIAL PRESS · NEW YORK

Text copyright © 1975 by Susan Pearson
Pictures copyright © 1975 by Diane Paterson
All rights reserved. First Printing
Printed in the United States of America
Typography by Atha Tehon

Library of Congress Cataloging in Publication Data
Pearson, Susan. Monnie hates Lydia.
[1. Brothers and sisters—Fiction.
2. Birthdays—Fiction]
I. Paterson, Diane, 1946– II. Title.
PZ7.P323316Mo [E] 75-9198
ISBN 0-8037-5443-4 ISBN 0-8037-5445-0 lib. bdg.

For Bill McKee

All week Monnie had been planning Lydia's birthday party. Lydia was Monnie's big sister, and she would be ten on Saturday. The party was a surprise, and Lydia didn't know a single thing about it.

But Monnie knew everything. Monnie knew that the party would be a picnic at Uncle Jack's lake in the country, and that the cake would be German chocolate, and that Uncle Jack had fixed up the old swanboat so they could all have rides. She and Daddy had sent out the invitations telling Lydia's friends it was a surprise party, they had wrapped the family presents and hidden them in the closet, and on Friday night, while Lydia was over at Toby's, they had baked the cake. Then they hid the cake in the closet too.

Saturday morning Monnie woke up early. She ran to Lydia's bed and pulled off the covers. "Wake up, Lydia! Wake up! It's your birthday!"

Lydia never woke up fast enough. She was grouchy. "Go away, Monnie," she said, and she pulled the covers back up and rolled over.

Monnie could hear the water running in the bathroom. Daddy was brushing his teeth.

"Lydia's cranky. She won't even get up on her birthday."

"Well, on her birthday I guess we can let Lydia sleep a little late," said Daddy between brushes. "Come help me make breakfast. She'll wake up when she smells the bacon."

"Well, Monnie, what should we fix for a birthday breakfast?" Daddy asked.

"Bacon and waffles and real orange juice," said Monnie. Waffles were Lydia's favorite breakfast. "And let's eat in the dining room with a tablecloth and the good dishes."

"Whatever you say, Mon. You fix the table, and I'll get started on the feast." Daddy tied on an apron, whistling "Clementine." Monnie liked how he always whistled while he cooked.

Monnie set the table with a pink tablecloth, the best dishes, and the pink goblets. It was a pink morning, she thought. Then she got the presents from the closet and put them at Lydia's place.

Just as everything was ready, Lydia walked in. Monnie figured she'd been watching from the doorway so she'd come in at exactly the right time.

"Happy birthday, sleepyhead," said Daddy, still in his doughy apron.

"Happy birthday, Lydia," said Monnie. "Open my present first!"

Lydia opened Daddy's present first. "Wow! My own easel! Thank you, Daddy!"

Then she opened Monnie's present.

"What is it?" she said.

"It's jars and turpentine and rags to clean up from painting," said Monnie. "And underneath that there's eight colors of real oil paints."

"Oh," said Lydia.

"Let's eat," said Daddy.

"Yippee!" Lydia shouted. "Waffles!" She didn't notice the fancy pink table.

After breakfast, while Lydia was getting dressed, Monnie and Daddy hid the picnic lunch and the beautiful German chocolate cake in the trunk of the car. They put the cake in an old hatbox and then put the hatbox in the middle of the spare tire, so the cake wouldn't get mashed on the way.

"Where are we going?" Lydia asked on their way out the door.

"It's a surprise!" said Monnie. "We're going to the country—to Uncle Jack's lake!"

"It's not a surprise if you tell me, dumbbell," Lydia said.

When they got to the lake, Lydia's four best friends were already there —Phyllis, Jean, Toby, and Barbara. Inside Uncle Jack's house they all changed into bathing suits. "Last one in the lake is *it* for water tag!" Daddy shouted. Monnie was last.

"I'm it!" Monnie yelled happily.

"It's no fun when *you're* it," Lydia complained. "You're too slow to catch anyone."

"Not when we're it together," said Daddy. "We'll catch every one of you." And they did, until Daddy quit to build the hot dog fire.

Then Lydia said, "Oh, Monnie, you're just in the way. Go help Daddy, why don't you."

"Look!" shouted Barbara. "What's that out in the lake?"

"It's a huge duck!" yelled Toby.

"It's a swan!" yelled Jean.

"It's Uncle Jack's swanboat!" Lydia shouted. "Come on!"

They scrambled up onto the dock, and Uncle Jack steered the boat next to them. "Climb aboard, girls," he said.

Lydia handed out the lifejackets: one to Phyllis, one to Toby, one to Jean, one to Barbara, and one for herself. Monnie was next—but there were no more jackets.

"You can't go out in the boat without a lifejacket, Monnie," Lydia said.

Monnie watched the swanboat pull away from the dock. "My sister's a real creep," she muttered to herself as she walked back up the hill.

Daddy's fire wasn't getting built very quickly. "Too much rain," he said. "Hard to find dry wood."

"I'll help you," Monnie said, and between the two of them they found just enough. Daddy lit the kindling, and then Monnie blew softly at the little flames until the larger pieces caught fire. By the time the boaters got back, chilly and wet, the fire was just right for warming up and roasting hot dogs.

Phyllis held her hands over the flames. "This sure feels good," she said.

"I blew on it to get it started," said Monnie.

"Big deal," said Lydia.

"Oh, leave her alone, Lydia," said Phyllis. "She's not so bad."

Lydia just laughed. "OK," she said, "but you wouldn't say that if she was *your* little sister."

Monnie put her roasted hot dog in a roll. "I'm gonna eat down on the dock," she told Daddy.

"All alone?" he asked.

"Just alone from Lydia," Monnie answered. "You can come if you want."

"I want," he said.

They carried their lunches to the lake.

"You know what, Daddy?" Monnie said. "I hate Lydia."

"Mmmm," Daddy answered. "She's a real stinker today."

"We could take her out on the boat and push her over and drown her," suggested Monnie.

"We'd get locked up in jail for that, though," said Daddy.

"Well—we could just beat her up then," said Monnie.

"We could," said Daddy, "but it wouldn't be fair two against one."

"Then just you could beat her up," said Monnie. "At least you could give her a spanking."

"Nope," said Daddy. "She hasn't been nasty to *me*. C'mon—let's go find the cake."

The cake was on the kitchen table. Daddy lit the candles. "You carry it out, Monnie," he said.

"Yuck," said Monnie.

"The more it bothers you, the meaner she'll be, Mon," said Daddy. "You've just got to be a good sport about it."

"Yeah," said Monnie. She picked up the cake very carefully and carried it outside.

Daddy sang "Happy Birthday to you," and everyone crowded around and sang too. Lydia blew out all the candles and everyone cheered.

"Hooray for Lydia!" Toby shouted.

"Hooray for the cake!" shouted Jean. "It looks yummy."

"*I* made it," Monnie said proudly.

"Oh, Monnie," said Lydia. "You just helped and you know it."

"I did too make it, Lydia," said Monnie very quietly. Being a good sport was hard with Lydia.

"Did not," answered Lydia very loudly as she pulled the candles out of the cake.

Monnie lifted the cake a little higher. "I don't care if it is your birthday, Lydia," she said. "If I've got to be a good sport, then so do you."

"I already am," said Lydia.

"Lydia," said Monnie, lifting the cake even higher, "I don't like you very much today." She moved the cake higher still, closer to Lydia's face.

Lydia stared at it as if she didn't really believe it was moving.

"You better be careful," she said. Monnie felt her own arms lifting the cake even closer . . . higher . . . closer . . . higher . . . closer . . . and then she mashed it right into Lydia's face.

Everybody stopped talking. Even Lydia didn't say anything. She just stared at Monnie.

Daddy handed Lydia a towel and kissed her on the cheek. "Well, good sport, you taste great," he said, and Phyllis giggled.

Lydia looked at Daddy. Then she looked at Monnie. Then she licked her face and shrugged her shoulders. "It's a good cake, Monnie," she said, and they all laughed and sat down on the ground and ate what was left of it with their fingers.

Susan Pearson

was born in Boston and grew up in Massachusetts, Virginia, and Minnesota. After her graduation from St. Olaf College, she worked for a year as a Vista Volunteer, then returned to Minnesota to become a Quaker Oats sales representative. In 1970 she came to New York City, where she is now a children's book editor. Ms. Pearson's first book, *Izzie*, was recently published. *Monnie Hates Lydia* is her second book.

Diane Paterson

was born in Brooklyn, New York. She has also lived in Colorado, Quebec, and Nova Scotia but now makes her home in Ridgefield, Connecticut, with her husband, who is an architect, and their two young daughters. Ms. Paterson studied at Pratt Institute and is the author-illustrator of *The Biggest Snowstorm Ever* and *Eat!*